Christmas 1984

for the Milton Childrens Christmases.
Have many "Happy" ones!

CHRISTMAS POEMS

CHRISTMAS POEMS

SELECTED BY
MYRA COHN LIVINGSTON

ILLUSTRATED BY
TRINA SCHART HYMAN

Holiday House / **New York**

For Matthew and Hillary

M.C.L.

Text copyright © 1984 by Myra Cohn Livingston
Illustrations copyright © 1984 by Trina Schart Hyman
All rights reserved
Printed in the United States of America
First Edition

Library of Congress Cataloging in Publication Data

Livingston, Myra Cohn.
Christmas poems.

Summary: Eighteen selections include offerings by
Harry Behn, X. J. Kennedy, Christina Rossetti, and
John Ciardi.
1. Christmas—Juvenile poetry. 2. Children's poetry.
[1. Christmas—Poetry] I. Hyman, Trina Schart, ill.
II. Title.
PN6110.C5L53 1984   808.81′933   83–18559
ISBN 0–8234–0508–7

CONTENTS

CHRISTMAS MORNING

Christmas bells, awake and ring
Your carol of long ago,
Awake O wintry sun and fling
Your beams across the snow!

Children, merrily merrily sing
That all the world may know
Today the angels earthward swing
To bless us here below!

HARRY BEHN

CHRISTMAS IS COMING

Christmas is coming, the geese are getting fat,
Please to put a penny in an old man's hat;
If you haven't got a penny, a ha'penny will do,
If you haven't got a ha'penny, God bless you.

Traditional, English

CHRISTMAS CHIME

Old lady in black bonnet,
    Bell she'd ting-a-ling——
I flung in half a dollar
    To hear her pot go *ping!*

Remembered then. Felt funny.
    Heart just started stopping.
I'd thrown away the money
    I had saved for shopping!

And yet my mother wasn't
    Mad. Called that *ping* of the pot
As merry a Christmas present
    As any she'd ever got.

X. J. KENNEDY

TINSEL

Not just its
Glittering furs
Draped over the
Tree's dark fingers,

Or its chill
Garlands of frost
Looped across every
Warm shop-window,

Nor even its sparks
Of ice in the
Prickly haloes
Of school-angels,

But its whisper
When lifted,
A sifting of
Silks and snows,

And its name,
Holding the faint
Silver tingle of its
Bristles: *tinsel.*

VALERIE WORTH

CANDY CANE

Hot wintry
Mint, striped
Round with
Fire and snow,

Sweet icicle
That melts
And burns
And chills,

And fills
The mouth with
Fumes of frost
And flame,

Crackling cold
On the tongue,
Like the word
Christmas.

VALERIE WORTH

COME CHRISTMAS

You see this Christmas tree all silver gold?
It stood out many winters in the cold,

with tinsel sometimes made of crystal ice,
say once a winter morning—maybe twice.

More often it was trimmed by fallen snow
so heavy that the branches bent, with no

one anywhere to see how wondrous is
the hand of God in that white world of his.

And if you think it lonely through the night
when Christmas trees in houses take the light,

remember how his hand put up one star
in this same sky so long ago afar.

All stars are hung so every Christmas tree
has one above it. Let's go out and see.

DAVID McCORD

ST. LUKE, 2:8-14

And there were in the same country shepherds
 abiding in the field, keeping watch over their
 flock by night.
And, lo, the angel of the Lord came upon them, and
 the glory of the Lord shone round about
 them: and they were sore afraid.
And the angel said unto them, Fear not: for, behold,
 I bring you good tidings of great joy, which
 shall be to all people.
For unto you is born this day in the city of David a
 Saviour, which is Christ the Lord.
And this shall be a sign unto you; Ye shall find the
 babe wrapped in swaddling clothes, lying in
 a manger.
And suddenly there was with the angel a multitude
 of the heavenly host praising God, and
 saying,
Glory to God in the highest, and on earth peace,
 good will toward men.

THE HOLY BIBLE
King James Version

CAROL OF THE BROWN KING

Of the three Wise Men
Who came to the King,
One was a brown man,
So they sing.

Of the three Wise Men
Who followed the Star,
One was a brown king
From afar.

They brought fine gifts
Of spices and gold
In jeweled boxes
Of beauty untold.

Unto His humble
Manger they came
And bowed their heads
In Jesus' name.

Three Wise Men,
One dark like me—
Part of His
Nativity.

LANGSTON HUGHES

"LOS PASTORES"

Let me tell to you the story
How I saw one night the shepherds,
Going walking, walking, walking
    To the manger in Belén.

Came one angel, very splendid,
With his white wings spread and shining,
Saying, "Hurry, shepherds, hurry,
    To the manger in Belén."

But then came the old *diablo,*
Splendid also in his red coat,
Saying, "Shepherds, do not hurry
    To the manger in Belén."

San Miguel, he fought the devil
With a long sword, swift and deadly;
So the shepherds went on walking
    To the manger in Belén.

One old shepherd was so sleepy
He lay down beside the roadway,
And they almost had to push him
    To the manger in Belén.

At the end of all the waiting
And the end of all the walking,
Last they found the Mother Mary
    With that carpenter, José.

Then they looked and looked in wonder
At the little Holy Baby;
And they all went kneeling, kneeling
    At the manger in Belén.

EDITH AGNEW

COME LEARN OF MARY

Who can't rejoice,
come learn of me
that hold a baby
on my knee,
and keep him safe
for what's to be.

Come, Joseph, share
a mother's pride.
Play with our boy
at seek, at hide.
Kneel, be a camel,
let him ride.

Let him recall,
in years to be,
should day grow dark,
too dark to see,
how once in light
we lived, we three.

NORMA FARBER

21

WHAT CAN I GIVE HIM?

What can I give Him
    Poor as I am?
If I were a shepherd
    I would bring a lamb,
If I were a Wise Man
    I would do my part,—
Yet what I can I give Him,
    Give my heart.

CHRISTINA ROSSETTI

CHRISTMAS PRAYER

(To be read very slowly out loud)

Children, tonight is for Santa—
For Santa who, year after year,
Familiar as redberry holly,
Is jolly St. Nick. He is here,

Convinced that the wide world, so troubling
In doubling not laughter, but woe,
Revolves like a pleasant old planet.
Oh, can it be? Answer is, No.

But let peace, though it fade by the minute,
Be in it—this room where we are;
Let the Saint from his chimney assemble
The symbols of tree, of bright star;

Of Christmas at dawn in a stocking,
Unlocking remembered delight
As it was. Praise Him, born in a stable,
At table: praise God. Bless this night.

DAVID McCORD

PHANTASUS: I, 8

On a mountain of sugar-candy,
under a blossoming almond-tree,
twinkles my gingerbread house.
Its little windows are of gold-foil, out of its chimney
steams wadding.

In the green heaven, above me, beams the Christmas-tree,

In my round sea of tinfoil
are mirrored all her angels, all her lights!

The little children stand about
and stare at me.

I am the dwarf Turlitipu.

My fat belly is made of gumdragon,
my thin pin-legs are matches,
my clever little eyes
raisins!

ARNO HOLZ
translated by Babette Deutsch

CHRISTMAS IN KEY WEST

I live in Key West where the pelicans play
And not even Santa could come in a sleigh.

He gets here, of course. For the last seven years
I have taken young Billy to meet him at Sears.

And I eavesdrop a bit. Well, not really eavesdropping,
But picking up hints for my own Christmas shopping.

And when I have listened, somehow, from somewhere,
Ho-ho-ho! and young Billy finds everything there—

All he wished for. Well, all I could find at the store.
And just to make sure, just a little bit more.

I can't say for certain how Santa gets there.
By glider, perhaps. Or by surfing on air

With dolphins hitched up to his board in the sky,
And pelicans wheeling to watch him skim by.

And when he has brought all that Billy was wishing,
The best part of Christmas is—we can go fishing,

Or sit by the pool when good friends come to call
And hear the bells ring MERRY CHRISTMAS TO ALL!

While Billy runs under the palm trees to play
With the stuff Santa brought for a warm Christmas Day.

Or we splash in the pool and we shout "Ho-ho-ho!
Now isn't this better than shoveling snow!"

JOHN CIARDI

THERE IS A YOUNG REINDEER
NAMED DONDER

There is a young reindeer named Donder,
Of whom Santa couldn't be fonder;
    But he falls off the roofs
    When his four little hoofs
Impatiently cause him to wander.

A WOMAN NAMED MRS. S. CLAUS

A woman named Mrs. S. Claus
Deserves to be heard from because
    She sits in her den
    Baking gingerbread men
While her husband gets all the applause.

two limericks by J. PATRICK LEWIS

27

KALEIDOSCOPE

Chock-full boxes, packages——
   squeeze 'em, feel sharp angles!
     From candycaned
     evergreen
       a tinfoil
       rainfall
           dangles.

Cold-tongued bells are tolling,
   tolling, *Hark, the herald*
     angels sing
     Christ the King!
       Earth's
       rebirth
          is caroled.

Sheep and ox guard manger
   Magi offer gifts.
     Down through white
     silent night
       slow
       snow
          sifts.

X. J. KENNEDY

A VISIT FROM ST. NICHOLAS

'Twas the night before Christmas, when all through the house
Not a creature was stirring, not even a mouse;
The stockings were hung by the chimney with care,
In hopes that St. Nicholas soon would be there;
The children were nestled all snug in their beds,
While visions of sugar-plums danced in their heads;
And mamma in her 'kerchief, and I in my cap,
Had just settled our brains for a long winter's nap—
When out on the lawn there arose such a clatter,
I sprang from my bed to see what was the matter.
Away to the window I flew like a flash,
Tore open the shutters, and threw up the sash.
The moon, on the breast of the new-fallen snow,
Gave the lustre of midday to objects below;
When, what to my wondering eyes should appear,
But a miniature sleigh and eight tiny reindeer,
With a little old driver, so lively and quick,
I knew in a moment it must be St. Nick.

More rapid than eagles his coursers they came,
And he whistled, and shouted, and called them by name:
"Now, *Dasher!* now, *Dancer!* now, *Prancer* and *Vixen!*
On, *Comet!* on, *Cupid!* on, *Donder* and *Blitzen!*
To the top of the porch! to the top of the wall!
Now dash away! dash away! dash away all!"
As dry leaves that before the wild hurricane fly,
When they meet with an obstacle, mount to the sky;
So up to the house-top the coursers they flew
With the sleigh full of toys, and St. Nicholas too.
And then, in a twinkling, I heard on the roof
The prancing and pawing of each little hoof—
As I drew in my head, and was turning around,
Down the chimney St. Nicholas came with a bound.
He was dressed all in fur, from his head to his foot,
And his clothes were all tarnished with ashes and soot;
A bundle of toys he had flung on his back,
And he looked like a pedlar just opening his pack.
His eyes—how they twinkled; his dimples, how merry!
His cheeks were like roses, his nose like a cherry!
His droll little mouth was drawn up like a bow,
And the beard of his chin was as white as the snow;
The stump of a pipe he held tight in his teeth,
And the smoke it encircled his head like a wreath;
He had a broad face and a little round belly
That shook, when he laughed, like a bowl full of jelly.
He was chubby and plump, a right jolly old elf,
And I laughed when I saw him, in spite of myself;
A wink of his eye and a twist of his head
Soon gave me to know I had nothing to dread;

He spoke not a word, but went straight to his work,
And filled all the stockings; then turned with a jerk,
And laying his finger aside of his nose,
And giving a nod, up the chimney he rose;
He sprang to his sleigh, to his team gave a whistle,
And away they all flew like the down of a thistle.
But I heard him exclaim, ere he drove out of sight,
"Happy Christmas to all, and to all a good night!"

CLEMENT CLARKE MOORE

ACKNOWLEDGMENTS

Grateful acknowledgment is made to the following poets, whose work was specially commissioned for this book:

John Ciardi for "Christmas in Key West." Copyright © 1984 by John Ciardi.

Norma Farber for "Come Learn of Mary." Copyright © 1984 by Norma Farber.

X. J. Kennedy for "Christmas Chime" and "Kaleidoscope." Copyright © 1984 by X. J. Kennedy.

J. Patrick Lewis for "There Is a Young Reindeer Named Donder" and "A Woman Named Mrs. S. Claus." Copyright © 1984 by J. Patrick Lewis.

David McCord for "Christmas Prayer." Copyright © 1984 by David McCord.

Valerie Worth for "Candy Cane." Copyright © 1984 by Valerie Worth.

Grateful acknowledgment is also made for the following reprints:

Farrar, Straus & Giroux, Inc., for "Tinsel" by Valerie Worth from *Small Poems Again.* Copyright © 1984 by Valerie Worth. Reprinted by permission of Farrar, Straus and Giroux, Inc.

Harcourt Brace Jovanovich, Inc., for "Christmas Morning" by Harry Behn from *Windy Morning.* Copyright 1953 by Harry Behn; renewed 1981 by Alice Behn Goebel, Pamela Behn Adam, Prescott Behn and Peter Behn. Reprinted by permission of Harcourt Brace Jovanovich, Inc.

The Horn Book Magazine for "Los Pastores" by Edith Agnew, reprinted from *The Horn Book Magazine* (November–December, 1937) © by The Horn Book, Inc.

Little, Brown and Company for "Come Christmas" by David McCord from *All Day Long.* Copyright © 1965 by David McCord. Reprinted by permission of Little, Brown and Company.

Harold Ober Associates for "Carol of the Brown King" by Langston Hughes from *The Crisis.* Copyright © 1958 by Crisis Publishing Company. Reprinted by permission of Harold Ober Associates Incorporated.